April

TO: Stella Grace

From: An admirer of yours!
Kathy Raneri

God Bless You ♡

Sophie's SPECIAL STORY

Gabriella Gizzo M.S., CCC-SLP, TSSLD

ISBN 979-8-88685-876-1 (hardcover)
ISBN 979-8-88685-875-4 (digital)

Christian Faith Publishing
832 Park Avenue
Meadville, PA 16335
www.christianfaithpublishing.com

This book is not intended as a substitute or in place of speech therapy, but rather to be used as a reliable resource.

This book is dedicated to: my parents, my siblings, and Sophie for all the love and support over the years.

Once upon a time, there was a **little** girl named Gabriella. Growing up, Gabriella was a little bit **quiet** and **shy** when it came to making friends.

In her neighborhood, Gabriella saw other children playing with puppies and saw how **happy** the puppies made them. She wanted a **little** puppy she could take care of.

As Gabriella grew, she enjoyed going on walks and running, and her love for dogs grew **stronger**. She knew she could take care of a puppy.

But it couldn't be just any puppy. It had to be the **best** puppy in the world. She soon learned that poodles are very **smart**, **fluffy**, and **easy** to train.

Gabriella and her family agreed that a poodle could be the **perfect** dog for her. They found a **blond** poodle puppy and brought her home.

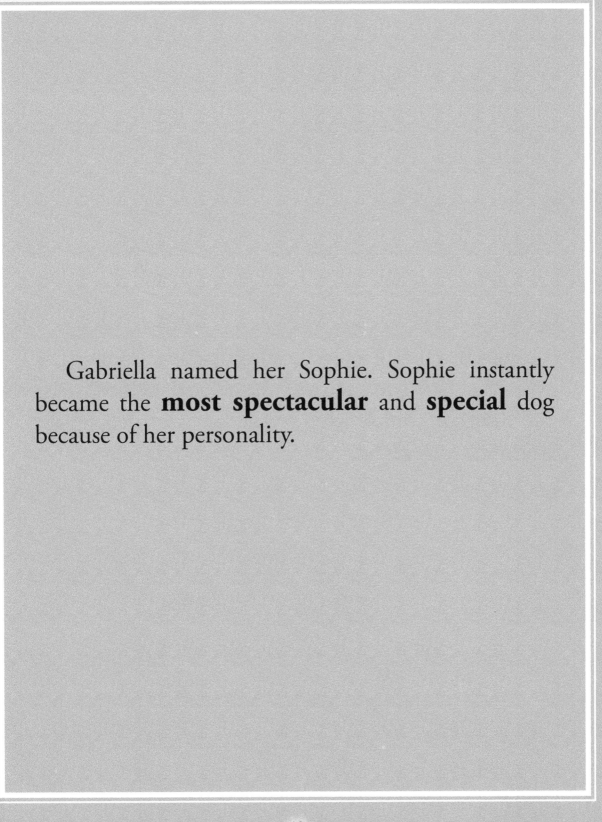

Gabriella named her Sophie. Sophie instantly became the **most spectacular** and **special** dog because of her personality.

Sophie was **full** of life, and she provided Gabriella with the **unconditional love** and **friendship** she wanted. Sophie would wake up Gabriella every morning with kisses.

They would do morning yoga together. They ate their meals together and exercised together. Gabriella's favorite part of the day was taking Sophie on walks in the neighborhood because Sophie gave smiles and kisses to everyone.

Everyone loved Sophie very much because she was **lovable** and **sociable** to everyone she met. Soon, Gabriella made friends in her neighborhood.

At the end of the day, Sophie would smile at Gabriella and would fall asleep on her lap.
Sophie had a big personality for a little dog.

Sophie was smart, sassy, snuggly, sleepy, spontaneous, sweet, sophisticated, stylish, and social, and she does the Sophie strut.

The End

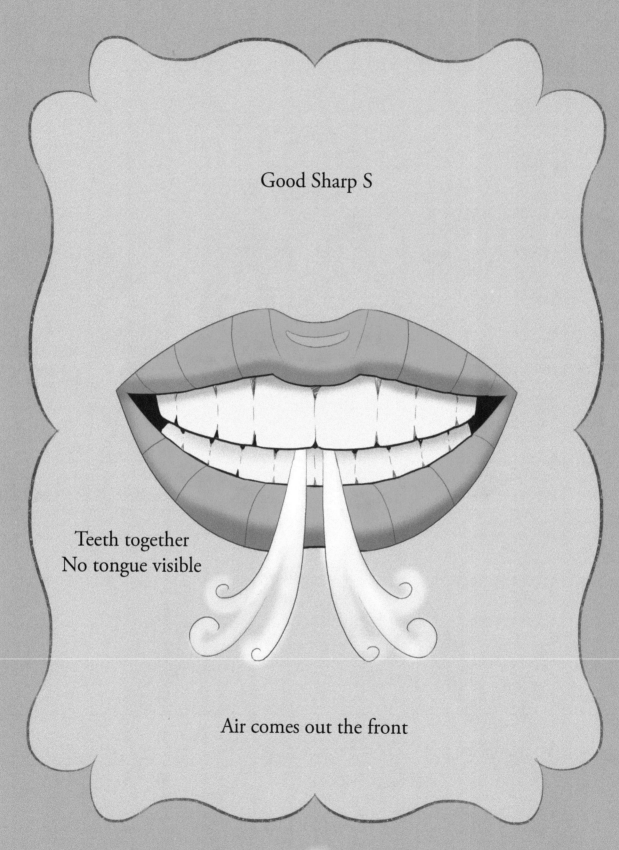

Good Sharp S

Teeth together
No tongue visible

Air comes out the front

Special Features

Verbal and visual tips for producing a strong /s/ sounds

1. Align your teeth with **gentle** closure in a smile.
2. Keep your tongue in your mouth, and let it relax on the floor of your mouth (keep the snake in the cage).
3. Produce the /s/ sound like in the word *Sophie*.
4. If you are trying to produce an /s/ cluster (e.g., **smart** or **sleepy**), first get your mouth ready by just focusing on the /s/ sound, then practice the next sound (e.g., /m/ or /l/). Finally, practice putting the two sounds together.

About the Author

Gabriella Gizzo is an author, daughter, sister, dog-lover, and speech language pathologist from Westchester, New York. Gabriella earned her bachelor of arts from Loyola University Maryland in speech language pathology/audiology. She then continued her studies at Adelphi University earning her master's of science in speech language pathology. Gabriella currently works with children ages three to fifteen years old with a variety of disabilities (e.g., autism, learning disabilities, speech language impairment, articulation, etc.) to meet their speech and language goals. In addition to her speech language pathology license, Gabriella also holds her teacher of students with speech and language disabilities (TSSLD). Her inspiration for writing this book is from combining her two passions in life: Sophie and speech language pathology. Gabriella is excited to share this story with the world because this unique story line will target a variety of speech and communication needs for any developing child.

CPSIA information can be obtained
at www.ICGtesting.com
Printed in the USA
BVHW011137070323
659868BV00007B/267